The
Spotty Dotty
Daffodil

For my dad, who taught me how to read.
Rose

To Fizzy, we miss you.
Love, Beth

The
Spotty Dotty
Daffodil

Written by Rose Mannering
Illustrated by Bethany Straker

Sky Pony Press
New York

When the daffodil was just a little bulb, he was planted in the garden with his brothers and sisters.

In spring they would all be bright yellow daffodils, and the little bulb could not wait.

All through the winter,
the little bulb slept in the
ground, warm and cozy.

When spring arrived, the little bulb woke up and started to stretch his roots. With the sun shining, the little bulb's brothers and sisters grew into tall daffodils with yellow flowers.

The other daffodils looked at their little brother, who was sneezing over and over again.

"What's wrong?" they asked him.

"And why do you have red spots on your petals?"

"I think—ACHOO!—I think I have a cold," the little daffodil said.

After a few days the little daffodil felt much better, but his spots did not go away.
"Why don't you look like the rest of us?" asked his brothers and sisters.
"You look very different."

The little daffodil's brothers and sisters grew taller and their beautiful yellow flowers shone like trumpets. They were the prettiest flowers in the garden.

"Oh, why do I have red spots?" cried the little daffodil. "I wish that I looked like everyone else."

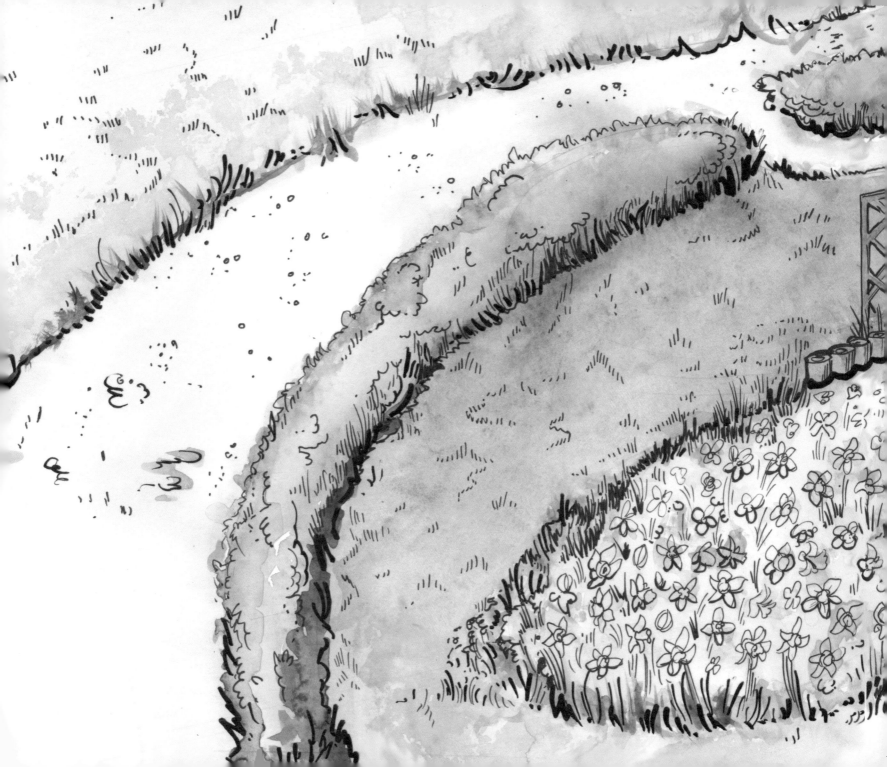

The next day, a little girl named Lucy came into the garden with her daddy.

The little daffodil tried
to hide, but Lucy spied
him right away.
"Look!" she gasped. "This
daffodil has red spots!"

"Why don't you choose a flower to bring inside and give to Nana?" said Daddy. "She needs some cheering up."

"This one!" cried Lucy, pointing at the little daffodil. "I've never seen a spotty dotty daffodil before. It's so pretty!"

Lucy carefully replanted the spotty dotty daffodil in a pot with Daddy's help. Then she took it inside to give to Nana.

"How rare!" said Nana. "Thank you, Lucy. This little daffodil makes me feel much better."

Nana placed the spotty dotty daffodil on the windowsill, and he waved at his brothers and sisters outside.

"Look at our little brother!" they all said. "See how lovely he looks with his red spots. I wish we all had spots like him."

Sky Pony Press books may be purchased in bulk at special discounts for sales promotion, corporate gifts, fund-
raising, or educational purposes. Special editions can also be created to specifications. For details, contact the
Special Sales Department, Sky Pony Press, 307 West 36th Street, 11th Floor, New York, NY 10018 or
info@skyhorsepublishing.com

Sky Pony® is a registered trademark of Skyhorse Publishing, Inc.®, a Delaware corporation.

Visit our website at www.skyponypress.com.

10 9 8 7 6 5 4 3 2 1

Manufactured in China, November 2013
This product conforms to CPSIA 2008

Library of Congress Cataloging-in-Publication Data

Mannering, Rose.
The spotty dotty daffodil / written by Rose Mannering ; illustrated by Bethany Straker.
pages cm
Summary: "A little daffodil blooms with spots all over his petals, which makes him different than his brothers and
sisters. But he soon learns that standing out can be quite rewarding"—Provided by publisher.
ISBN 978-1-62636-346-5 (hardback)
[1. Daffodils--Fiction. 2. Individuality—Fiction. 3. Self-acceptance—Fiction.] I. Straker, Bethany, illustrator. II.
Title.
PZ7.M31518Sp 2014
[E]—dc23
2013035690